E   Tafuri, Nancy.
Taf   Have you seen my
            duckling?

DATE DUE		PERMA-BOUND	
		MAR 17	
		APR 17 1987	
	MAR 8 1995		

D1370224

Have You Seen My Duckling?

Nancy Tafuri

Puffin Books

PUFFIN BOOKS
Viking Penguin Inc., 40 West 23rd Street, New York, New York 10010, U.S.A.
Penguin Books Ltd, Harmondsworth, Middlesex, England
Penguin Books Australia Ltd, Ringwood, Victoria, Australia
Penguin Books Canada Limited, 2801 John Street, Markham, Ontario, Canada L3R 1B4
Penguin Books (N.Z.) Ltd, 182–190 Wairau Road, Auckland 10, New Zealand

First published by Greenwillow Books 1984
Published in Picture Puffins 1986
Reprinted 1986

Copyright © Nancy Tafuri, 1984
All rights reserved

Library of Congress Cataloging in Publication Data
Tafuri, Nancy.   Have you seen my duckling?
Summary: A mother duck leads her brood around
the pond as she searches for one missing duckling.
[1. Lost children—Fiction.   2. Ducks—Fiction.   3. Ponds—Fiction]   I. Title.
PZ7.T117Hav   1986   [E]   85-43129   ISBN 0-14-050585-7

Printed in U.S.A.
by Rae Publishing Co., Inc., Cedar Grove, New Jersey

Early one morning...

Have you
seen my
duckling?

Have you seen my duckling?

Have
you seen
my duckling?

Have you seen my duckling?

Have you
seen my
duckling"